Mr. N...s
Meets the Tooth Fairy

Carmel Trovato

Illustrated by
Sierra Mon Ann Vidalt

Print information available on the last page

Rev. date: 06/25/2019

To order additional copies of this book, contact:
Xlibris
1-800-455-039
www.xlibris.com.au
Orders@Xlibris.com.au

Mr. Nibbles
Meets the Tooth Fairy

Carmel Trovato

Illustrated by
Sierra Mon Ann Vidalt

Once upon a time, there was a little mouse that nibbled on everything he could put his teeth in. He nibbled on cheese. He nibbled on shoes. He nibbled on chairs and even on stools. There was nothing that he wouldn't try to nibble on. For this very reason, the farm animals called him "Mr. Nibbles."

Mr. Nibbles lived out in the barn with all the other farm animals. Even if he was only a tiny little mouse and all the other animals were bigger and stronger than he was, they all feared him.

"Why did they fear him?" you might ask. Because during the night, when all the animals were asleep, Mr. Nibbles might decide to nibble on their feet.

Mr. Nibbles was very adventurous and very curious. By now he'd already nibbled on everything in the barn and was looking for something new.

Now where else could he look? Maybe you already know. Yes! Outside the barn there must be somewhere to go.

Mr. Nibbles nibbled his way out of the barn. Now he stood astounded and amazed outside under the moonlight. The moon looked like cheese up there in the sky, but it was too far for him to bite. But only a short distance away, he noticed a light coming from inside a house.

Mr. Nibbles thought, *That's where I'll go nibbling tonight!*

He invited himself in, squeezing under the door. Once inside, he was surprised to find no hay on the floor.

What a lovely place! he thought. *No place I'd rather be. There are so many things here for me to see. Tonight I can nibble on something new instead of that usual worn-out shoe.*

Upstairs, Mr. Nibbles thought. *That's where I'll go.* But suddenly, he froze when someone called out, "Joe!"

"Joe, Joe," said a voice. "Go downstairs and look!"

"Oops," Mr. Nibbles exclaimed. "They must have heard me nibbling on that book."

Mr. Nibbles panicked and fled into a room to escape from Joe and that wicked broom. He dared not breathe from under a bed until all was quiet, and then he fled. He ran into a cupboard and into a box where lots of toys awaited him, even some socks.

A box full of treasures for him to explore—dolls, plastic cups and saucers, and one brass bell that he bit into so eagerly his tooth fell.

"Oh, dear me," Mr. Nibbles said with a sob. "I can't return to the barn and face that mob."

All the barn animals would laugh at him until they'd turn blue, so he stayed in the house to look for some glue. No glue in the cupboards, on tables, or in drawers, nor in coat pockets and trousers. He found nothing at all.

It was late, and Mr. Nibbles looked for somewhere safe to spend the night without being seen. Inside a wardrobe he saw a green hat.

Great! he thought. *Tonight I shall sleep in that.*

Just before he fell asleep, he looked through a keyhole because he heard the voice of a little girl speaking to her doll. The little girl held a small tooth in the palm of her hand and said to her doll, "You see this tooth of mine? It's been wobbling for quite some time. Tonight, the tooth fairy will be here, and I think she'll be all dressed in pink."

"How wonderful, the tooth fairy!" Mr. Nibbles exclaimed. "I wonder if she's big or if she's small. I can't miss this scene at all!"

Mr. Nibbles had no idea of who the tooth fairy was. After all, he'd been living out in the barn with all the other animals, and they never mentioned tooth fairies.

Mr. Nibbles was so excited. All night he kept looking through the keyhole, spying on the little girl and her doll. Just before the little girl went to bed, he listened carefully to what she said.

"Now, my little princess, it's time for you to sleep. Now don't you try to peep, or the tooth fairy won't come when I'm fast asleep."

Her tooth lay on the set of drawers beside her bed. It was a tiny white tooth, but Mr. Nibbles's tooth was even tinier that hers.

Soon, all was clear. And when no one could hear, Mr. Nibbles went into her room and placed his tooth beside hers. He hid behind the lampshade and waited.

Suddenly, in the distance, Mr. Nibbles saw a shimmering light. This light looked like a star but wasn't as far. Then it whirled and it twirled and shaped into a girl. She had wings, of course, because all fairies do. And the little girl was right; she was wearing pink too. She was not very big, as small as a mouse, and flickered so brightly inside the house.

The tooth fairy carried a silver bag and a gold bag. She picked up the girl's tooth and placed it in the silver bag. Then she reached inside the gold bag and took out a coin, placing it on the set of drawers where her tooth had been.

Then the tooth fairy noticed the much smaller tooth beside the coin. She picked it up and wondered whose it could be. "Oh, now I know," she said, realising Mr. Nibbles's presence.

"Come out, little one. I won't hurt you. You did right to wait. I can help you, you know."

Mr. Nibbles stepped out from behind the lampshade and walked towards her ray of light. He was still astonished and amazed for he had not foreseen this sight.

The tooth fairy said, "You're a good and brave little mouse. Today I'll reward you with a new tooth made just for you."

So she waved her glittering wand, and in a short while, a new tooth appeared on Mr. Nibbles's smile.

"I can't thank you enough," Mr. Nibbles said, feeling shame. "For this mishap of mine, I am only to blame."

Mr. Nibbles looked curiously at the silver bag, in which the tooth fairy collected all the children's little white teeth, and asked indiscreetly, "Why do you collect all these?"

The tooth fairy explained, "Just like silver and gold, these are treasures to hold. They give us the spirit of children, their goodness, their innocence, and their benevolence."

Mr. Nibbles then noticed the beaded white teeth shaped into pearls around the tooth fairy's neck and wrists, which she wore just like jewels.

"Now my good and brave little friend, if I have your permission, I will send you on an important mission."

The tooth fairy explained that in many parts of the world, instead of fairies collecting children's teeth, there are little mice to help do her job.

"I'd be proud to make you an honourable member of our team," she told Mr. Nibbles.

"So when each child is asleep, and make sure they don't peep, you can leave them a coin for their tooth while they're fast asleep."

Mr. Nibbles felt honoured and promised to be loyal and true. Curious as his nature was, Mr. Nibbles had to ask one last question. "Oh, tooth fairy, dear, I'm so curious to know. Who makes all these wonderful jewels?"

"Why, of course." She smiled and replied, "I thought you knew. It's all little mice just like you."

CPSIA information can be obtained at www.ICGtesting.com
Printed in the USA
BVIW122004050719
552612BV00030B/45